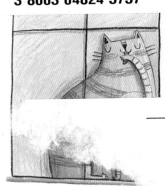

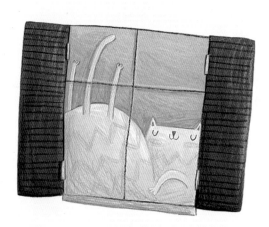

For my husband

First published in 2017 by Child's Play (International) Ltd
Ashworth Road, Bridgemead, Swindon SN5 7YD, UK

Published in USA by Child's Play Inc
250 Minot Avenue, Auburn, Maine 04210

Distributed in Australia by Child's Play Australia Pty Ltd
Unit 10/20 Narabang Way, Belrose, Sydney, NSW 2085

ISBN 978-1-84643-933-9
CLP221216CPL02179339

Printed in Shenzhen, China

1 3 5 7 9 10 8 6 4 2

A catalogue record of this book
is available from the British Library

www.childs-play.com

All About Cats

Monika Filipina

This book is ALL about cats.
Cats spend the whole day sleeping in a chair.
Or do they?

Our human's gone!
What shall we do now?

I've got
a plan...

So have I!

Dancing?

Skating?

Reading?

Phew! That was tiring. Time for a snooze.
Squeeze in, stretch out. Curl around, squash up.

Sweet dreams...

Snack time!

Measuring, chopping,
stirring and whisking!
Mmmm, tastes good!

Smile please.

How do I look in this?

Where am I?

Breathe in!

Eeeeeek!

Let's curl up
with a good book.

How do you spell 'sardines'?

Come on in!
The water's lovely!

Look at me. I'm a Ninja!

Oo-ar! Where's that pirate treasure?

Come on everybody, let's see you dance!

Painting, shaping, pasting, sculpting, drawing.
So creative! We love art.

Shhhhh! Leave us in peace, we're playing chess.

Roll up, roll up!

Come and watch
the acrobats!

Shhhhh!
Our human's back!

Didn't we have fun?
And no one will ever know.

Or will they?